Antis and t[illegible] e

Ankit

Published by Sahitya press, 2024.

ANTIS AND THE GREAT BUG BATTLE

First edition. September 15, 2024.

Written by Ankit.

Table of Contents

Title Page

Copyright Page

Dedication

Preface

Antis and the Great Bug Battle

Moral of the story

Sign up for Ankit's Mailing List

Further Reading: The Lost Baby Lion

Also By Ankit

For young readers

Preface

Dear Readers,

I am delighted to present to you

Antis: A Poor Ant Size Boy This

tale of courage, patience, and self-discovery was inspired by the idea that no matter how small we may feel in this vast world, each one of us has a purpose. Antis, the tiny boy, may seem insignificant at first glance, but his journey from feeling lost and purposeless to becoming a leader and protector of an entire city is a testament to the strength we all carry within us.

Through the adventures of Antis, I wanted to emphasise that greatness is not determined by size, but by the courage we show in the face of challenges. Antis's story reminds us that we all have something unique to offer, and it is often in the moments of our greatest doubt that we discover our true strength.

I hope this story brings joy, inspiration, and hope to readers of all ages, and that Antis' journey helps you realise that you, too, can make a difference—no matter how small you may feel.

Yours

Ankit Kirar

Antis and the Great Bug Battle

In a small village, far from the hustle and bustle of big cities, lived a boy named Antis. But Antis was not like other boys. He was so small that his height and build were equal to that of an ant. No one in the village knew who he was or where he came from. He had no family, no friends, and lived completely alone. He was so small that no one had ever seen him.

Antis spent his days thinking, "Why am I so small? Why was I even born? Why did God make me?" These questions weighed heavily on his heart. He felt as if he was useless, as if his life had no meaning.

Every day, he would eat, sleep, and do his chores, but his sadness never left him. He would watch the people of the village, who were much taller than him, laugh, play, and work, but no one had ever seen him. After all, he was the size of an ant.

One day, Antis was sitting outside his small house on the soft grass. He saw ants passing by him. They always seemed busy, always doing something important. Antis understood that even though he was a human, the ants seemed more important than him in this world.

"Why did you make me so small, God? Why are you so cruel? I can't do anything in this world. I'm of no use. Everyone is doing something; everyone has a purpose in life, but you created me for no reason. If I were tall and strong like other humans, I would rule this world. But now I'm alone. I am small." He started crying.

Just then, a few ants stopped near him. He didn't pay attention, thinking they were just regular ants going for their work. But when they didn't go further and saw him crying, he yelled, "Go away, don't bother me, you have a lot of work to do, so go do it, leave me alone."

But these ants were different. They looked at him as if they wanted to say something. They were scared, but one of them gathered courage and, in a small voice, said, "Antis! We need your help!"

Antis was surprised. How could he help anyone? He wiped his tears and looked at the ants;

they were serious. They were very sad. They really needed help.

He bent down, his small size making him almost eye-level with the ants.

"Help? How can I help? I'm so small. No one even knows me," Antis said.

The ants looked at each other and then at him. "You are small like us, but you are human. You can do what we can't. Our city is in danger! We ants are in danger. A big, terrifying, and very large bug eats us ants and destroys everything. It has destroyed many of our cities, many ant kingdoms. We can't do anything in front of it, it is very powerful. We need your help to stop it!"

Antis thought for a moment. He had never done anything

important in his life, but here were these ants, asking him for help, who were very sad. Maybe, just maybe, this was his chance to prove that he wasn't useless.

"I will help you," Antis said, standing up as tall as he could, given his size. The ants jumped with joy. Seeing their happiness, he too felt happiness.

He was not useless anymore. He locked his small house and went along with the ants to help them. The ants started leading him to their city. Ants live underground.

Antis followed the ants and reached a small hole, which was just the right size for him to crawl into. As soon as he entered, what he saw amazed him.

The underground ant city was beautiful! There were round

tunnels, tiny sand houses, and thousands of ants working together. Some were bringing food, some were guarding the city, and so on.

The ants introduced Antis to their queen, who was a wise and kind ruler.

"Thank you for coming to help us," she said kindly, "Our city has lived peacefully for many years, but now that terrible bug that eats us ants is coming to destroy everything we have built, it will come to kill all of us. We are small, but we are many. Still, without someone like you, we won't be able to stop it."

For the first time in his life, Antis felt very important. He realised his own strength. He spent the next two days learning about the ants, understanding their city and their lives. He was happy living among them and felt a peace he had never felt before.

But on the third day, disaster struck. The ant-eating bug

attacked the city, its large jaws chewing through tunnels and homes, destroying them.

In no time, it had completely wiped out the eastern part of

the city, and many ants were killed as the bug ate them all up quickly. In just a few minutes, half the ant population was gone. Once the bug was full, it left.

Antis saw the bug's destruction in the city. He wanted to help, but he didn't know how. After all, he was just a small human. How could he stop something so big and powerful? The bug was much larger and stronger than Antis.

That night, Antis couldn’t sleep. He felt like he had let the ants down.

"I couldn’t do my job. The ants had hope in me. Their hopes are crushed, but that bug was so big, how could I fight it? How will I defeat it?" He kept thinking.

As he thought more, an idea came to his mind, "I may be

small, but I am also a human. I have intelligence, and I can use it to fight that bug."

The next day, Antis got to work. He collected some things from the village – a sharp needle, a piece of thread, a blade, and some sticky tree sap. He made a powerful weapon, strong enough to defeat the ant-eating bug.

He tested the weapon and found it to be even more dangerous than he had imagined. With it, he could kill that big ant-eating bug. All the ants were happy with Antis's preparations.

While talking among themselves, they said that Antis was very wise.

At night, Antis went to sleep in his room in the queen's palace in the ant city. He had a good sleep. But as morning was about to break, the ant-eating bug returned.

The bug began causing even more destruction. Antis was woken up, and he was ready. He picked up his weapon and bravely stood in front of the palace doors, holding the weapon he had made.

The bug ran towards him quickly, its jaws opening wide and terrifyingly. But Antis was quick. In one swift move, he stabbed the bug's hands with the sharp needle. The bug roared in pain and started thrashing around. The bug had never expected this.

Before it could rise again, Antis wrapped the thread around the bug’s legs, tying it up completely so it couldn’t move. The bug was caught. Seeing this, all the ants and the queen came outside. Their fear was gone. Watching them, Antis asked, "What should we do, should we kill this bug or..."

Before Antis could say anything more, all the ants started shouting,

"Kill, kill this sinful bug."

Then, with one final strike, Antis, in front of everyone, cut off the ant-eating bug's neck, killing it.

All the ants were filled with joy and ran towards Antis. They lifted him up on their tiny hands and started cheering,
"Long live Antis, long live Antis."
Antis felt proud of himself. He had never felt this way before.

He was being carried around the city on the ants' hands. All the ants were looking at him with respect, as if he were a god. He had saved their city!

The ant queen declared,

"Antis, you have saved all our lives. From now on, you will be our king. You may be small, but you have a sharp mind, a big heart, and great courage."

From that day, Antis became the king of the ants and ruled over them. He began living in their beautiful underground city, among friends who loved and respected him.

The ants helped him, and he became the most powerful person in the world, becoming the king of the world. With the help of the ants, he began influencing the whole world.

He still lives under the earth. Everyone knows him. Everyone fears him. If anyone anywhere kills an ant, Antis attacks them with his army.

He had learned that being small doesn't mean being weak. Everything has a purpose, just like he had one. And it was much bigger than he had ever thought.

He found happiness, strength, and meaning in his life. He had become the god of the ants and still lives beneath the earth. Long live Antis.

LONG LIVE ANTIS,

Moral of the story

No matter how small you are, God has a plan for you. Be patient, and never think you are too small to make a difference.

Don't miss out!

Click the button below and you can sign up to receive emails whenever Ankit publishes a new book. There's no charge and no obligation.

https://books2read.com/r/B-A-MZXJB-NVYZE

Connecting independent readers to independent writers.

Did you love *Antis and the Great Bug Battle*? Then you should read *The Lost Baby Lion* by Ankit!

Join Singha, **a curious baby lion,** on an unforgettable adventure deep within the jungle! What starts as an **innocent mistake**

quickly turns into a **life-changing challenge** as Singha strays too far from home and falls into the **clutches of cunning jackals.** Trapped and made to serve as **their slave**, Singha feels powerless—until he remembers his true nature. With newfound courage, he rises up to reclaim his rightful place as **the king of the jungle!**

"The Lost Baby Lion" is an exciting and heartwarming tale for children **aged 6-9**, filled with **beautiful illustrations** that bring the jungle to life. This engaging story teaches kids valuable lessons about **self-belief, bravery,** and the importance of never forgetting who they are, even in the face of life's toughest challenges.

With captivating storytelling and an **inspiring moral** at its core, this book is perfect for **bedtime reading** or as a gift for young readers who love **adventure and animals**. Watch your child's imagination soar as they follow Singha's journey from fear to triumph, reminding them to always stand tall and be **courageous—just like a lion!**

Get your copy today and let the adventure begins!

Also by Ankit

Dhruv Stran

Dhruv Stran in Unknown Space : A Science Fiction Children's Novel

Panchatanra Stories

Kids Short Stories : 21 Panchtantra Stories for Children

Moral Stories : 28 Illustrated Bedtime Stories for Children

Children's Stories: 27 Illustrated Bedtime Stories for Kids

Sharthak in space

Lost in Space: A Superhero Born - A Science Fiction Novel

Three days three seasons

A Day in India : Account of 26 November 2024

Standalone

5-Minute Bedtime Stories: 45 Illustrated Moral Tales, Short Stories, and Fables for Kids

The True Story of Ah Q & The Diary of a Madman

Moral Stories : 14 Illustrated Bedtime Stories for Kids

Beyond the Stars: The Galactic Battle for Survival

Bedtime Stories: 30 Illustrated Short Stories for Kids

81 Bed time Stories (Illustrated) - Story Book for Kids

The Aliens : Trapped in the Bushes - A Science Fiction Moral Story

Into the Space: Collection of Four Science Fiction Books

The Story of Poor Farmer

Short Stories of Panchatantra: Moral Stories and Bedtime Stories for Kids

The Little Bird Who Dreamed to Fly

The Adventure of Fairy Ben and Little Ankit

Monty : The Sporting Monkey

A Snake Incident and Other Stories from India

The Lost Baby Lion

Antis and the Great Bug Battle

Milton Keynes UK
Ingram Content Group UK Ltd.
UKHW022054260924
448786UK00012B/541